Luke Blake's Screenplay

Barrie David

Published by Barrie David, 2023.

LUKE BLAKE'S SCREENPLAY

First edition. July 15, 2023.

ISBN: 979-8223469797

Written by Barrie David.

To my wife Elly...

Thanks for forty three amazing years...

Also Ajax and Support Team at D2D for their help...

'Luke Blake's Screenplay'
Barrie David
SUNRISE - ARIZONA INTERIOR - YESTERDAY...
Amid a backdrop of mountainous desert terrain the rising sun
provides a spectacular display of intermingling copper and gold clouds,
when they slowly fade to an infinity of clear blue sky the rugged
landscape, silent and still, is dominated by searing merciless heat.
CUT TO - An American Eagle, gliding majestically above a remote
mountain range gazes down at a stationary Recreational Vehicle on a
narrow mountain trail that's crudely hand painted in military combat
green and coated with the grime of extensive mileage. The RV has a
steel rack above the cab roof and a pull-out sunshade which is not in
use. A sliding side door is slightly open. Near the RV is a cluster of
massive boulders.
CUT TO - A small, semi dark bedroom in the RV showing a floor to
ceiling storage cupboard with sliding doors. In front of the cupboard
are two sets of top and bottom bunks. On a top bunk, a man in his
mid-thirties, six feet tall and ruggedly handsome, is sound asleep.
A brief screen message shows he's Jeffrey Blake.
CUT TO - On a top bunk opposite Jeffrey sleeps a teenage boy whose
deep suntan sits well with his mass of blonde curly hair.
A screen message shows – he's Jeffrey's son, Luke.
CUT TO - In the narrow gap between two lower bunks lays a
slumbering medium sized black and white mongrel. A screen message
shows his name is Beric.
CUT TO - The Eagle. Circling the RV, intently watching dozens of
reptiles that emerge from a dark crevice between the boulders.
Suddenly plummeting down, with breath-taking precision it scoops up
a small rattlesnake from the crest of one of the boulders. With
predator and prey a distant airborne dot...
SCENES FADES...
NEW SCENE – THE BEDROOM.

CUT TO – While Jeffrey and Luke continue to sleep Beric stirs, briefly yawns and plods over to a large circular stainless-steel bowl near the base of the storage cupboard. The vague sound as he laps up what water remains in the bowl is the only challenge to the absolute silence. Returning to the lower bunks Beric settles down, but suddenly alert, moves to the closed bedroom door. Sniffing around the base he rears up and begins forcefully scratching the door. The sound does not awaken Jeffrey, but Luke, sitting up and grinning how Beric pleads to relieve himself, promptly sweeps back his bedding and climbs down from his bunk. Naked except for boxer shorts, Luke proves to be tall and well-built. Combined with his suntan and blonde curly hair his piercing china blue eyes show him to be an extraordinarily handsome young man. The instant Luke opens the bedroom door, Beric surges passed him into the main area of the RV, the lounge where three rattlesnakes, coiled up beside a narrow gap in the side door, collectively attack Beric when he approaches them. In the blink of an eye the absolute silence is shattered by a chilling crescendo of vicious barking and frenzied rattling. The horrifying scene is conveyed via Luke's bulging terrified eyes as he sees the un-survivable plight of Beric and to retrieve him would be suicidal. In stark panic Luke turns and retreats into the bedroom, slamming the door with such force it rebounds wide open as he frantically scrambles up to his bunk.

CUT TO - Jeffrey, rapidly sitting up in his bunk, gazing in horrified disbelief from Luke, visibly trembling on the opposite bunk, to the lounge to see Beric, panting heavily as he slumps to the floor. Staring down from their bunks, father and son instinctively recoil as they watch one of the deadly snakes rapidly slithers from the lounge into the bedroom, its hideous rattle rasping on nerve endings of man and boy when it halts in a writhing aggressive coil between the two lower bunks a mere four feet below them...

SCENE FADES STATING THREE WEEKS EARLIER...

NEW OPENING SCENE

SOUTHBOUND FREEWAY
PHOENIX – ARIZONA.

CUT TO - Aerial view showing a Freeway with traffic of every size and description.

CUT TO – The cab of an antiquated Pickup Truck lumbering along the inside lane and an elderly overweight man of Hispanic appearance who gazes anxiously at a gauge on the dashboard indicating fuel is close to zero. Fumbling for a packet of cigarettes the man shakes one loose and lights it with the remains of a cigarette he's already smoking. Glancing in his rear-view mirror he sees an Arizona Police Cruiser behind him. The drone of the engine suddenly fades causing traffic behind to brake as the Pickup rolls to a halt. With its blue flashing lights and its siren wailing the police cruiser halts behind the Pickup, its two-man crew exiting to take control as the inside lane begins backing up.

CUT TO - The rear of the tailback where a red Ferrari draws to a halt. Jeffrey Blake steps from the cab to glimpse the long line of traffic in front of him. Slumping back into the driving seat he pulls the door closed and with obvious gloom stares at a six-by-six picture glued to the dashboard showing a soldier wearing a 1940's American army uniform depicting on the left shoulder the head of an eagle with the word. 'Airborne'. The base of the picture shows the wording.

Sergeant George Blake. 101st Airborne Division.
Killed - December 1944 at Bastogne

Sighing heavily, Jeffrey begins watching a man and a teenage boy who climb down from a stationary RV in front of him to examine a rear tyre. Wearing tee shirts, trainers, and shorts showing shards of cotton where they've been crudely severed from a pair of jeans, they hurriedly return to the RV when their lane begins to move.

CUT TO - The cruiser crew, halting central traffic for vehicles in the blocked lane to pass the motionless Pickup truck.

CUT TO - The Ferrari. Jeffrey, now on the open road, nodding thoughtfully as he accelerates passed the man and boy in the lumbering RV.

SCENE FADES...
NEW OPENING SCENE STATING – JEFFREY'S PALATIAL HOME.

Showing the Ferrari moving down a lengthy driveway bordered by white picket fencing toward a large ranch style house, a vast forecourt with a huge double garage and a generous front veranda with multiple chairs, tables, and sun loungers. A brief aerial view of the rear of the house shows a swimming pool, a Sauna, a Jacuzzi, and shower cubicles.

CUT TO - Parking beside a Mercedes Coupe Jeffrey scoops up his jacket and a briefcase and strides briskly to the house. Echoing from the house is gentle, immensely captivating piano playing.

CUT TO - Jeffrey, crossing a marble-floored reception hallway dominated by a wide mahogany stairway then entering a spacious lounge boasting oak flooring randomly dotted with exquisite hand-woven Persian rugs. Nestling in front of a wide stone fireplace two large white leather settees in no way contrast with the surrounding period furniture. At the far end of the lounge, in front of glazed cantilevered doors overlooking the rear garden, a stunningly beautiful blonde-haired woman wearing pale blue jeans and a red cotton shirt plays a Steinway Grand Piano. A screen heading shows she's Jeffrey's wife Elena. (Nickname Lenny).

Pausing as she watches Jeffrey offload his coat and briefcase onto a Regency Chair, Lenny briefly smiles when Jeffrey comments.

"Don't stop Len! I love what you do with that piano!"

Lenny resumes playing. Jeffrey walks to a well-stocked cocktail bar fronted by a row of bar stools. Moments later Lenny settles onto one.

LENNY - Pleasantly inquiring.

"How's your day been?"
JEFFREY - Engrossed in making drinks.
"A truck broke down on the Freeway, it was chaos until the cops got
things moving!"
JEFFREY- Brusquely enquiring.
"Where's Luke?"
LENNY – Informatively.
"In his bedroom!"
JEFFREY- Sarcastically as he places a drink for Lenny on the bar.
"Where he goes every time I come home!"
LENNY – Affirmatively.
"Let's not go there Jeff, we'll only argue!"
JEFFREY - Retorting.
"We could try talking without arguing!"
LENNY- Knowingly.
"When it comes to Luke we always argue, we go around in circles, I tell
you about your indifference to him and your obsession for profit, you
never fail to justify yourself, and nothing changes!"
JEFFREY - Persistently.
"Profit pays for this house, the cars, the Caribbean cruises, and
everything Luke wants, but we can't be in the same room without
something kicking off..."
LENNY – Impatiently.
"Another full circle! What's on your mind Jeff? Where is this headed?"
JEFFREY- Staring down at his drink.
"I've got an idea that might resolve things with me and Luke?"
LENNY – Curiously.
"Go on!"
JEFFREY – Informatively.
"I want to take him on a man-to-man vacation in an RV, the idea is box
him up with nowhere to go, we're sure to argue and hopefully clear the
air once and for all!"

JEFFREY – Watching Lenny closely as he continues.

"If I ask him, he will dig in before I even finish speaking and nothing will budge him! If anyone can persuade him to go with me, you can!"

LENNY – Immediately critical as she retorts.

"I've been telling you for years to spend more time with Luke, but you never listened, the terrible atmosphere between you is not Luke's fault! It might surprise you he's a great kid!"

JEFFREY – Affirmatively.

"I'm listening now! Will you talk to him?"

LENNY - Hesitating, before answering.

"Your idea can't make things any worse than they already are so yes, I'll talk to him later this evening, but I know exactly how he's going to react!"

JEFFREY - Leaning forward to briefly touch his glass to hers. "That's all I ask!"

SCENE FADES

NEW SCENE – LATER THAT EVENING

CUT TO - Lenny, walking up the mahogany stairway, crossing the landing to a door showing an A4 print out saying in large bold lettering. **'Luke's Sanctuary'**

Lenny gently knocks the door. A gruff boyish voice abruptly demands.

"Who is it?"

LENNY - Pensively.

"Need to speak to you Luke?"

Luke Blake opens the door.

LUKE. Amenably.

"Hey Mom! What's happening?"

With a brief half smile Lenny settles on Luke's bed and gazes at a large all-in-one computer resting on a solid oak desk. The screen shows the Roman Colosseum. On a swing-out bracket beside the desk a fifty-inch LG television is not turned on and hangs like a dormant blank picture. Two walls have shelves showing rows of CD's and books about

Movie Stars. A further wall shows a montage of actors who have starred in epic films about ancient Rome. Richard Burton The Robe - Victor Mature Demetrius and the Gladiators - Charlton Heston Ben Hur - Kirk Douglas Spartacus - Russell Crowe Gladiator – Channing Tatum – The Eagle. It's the bedroom of a rich kid who obviously loves movies.

LENNY - Nodding at the computer screen.

"What are you working on?"

LUKE - With boyish enthusiasm.

"We're doing a competition in School, it's called Movie Idea, it's to see who can write the best screenplay! I've started a story about a soldier who joins the Roman Army, did you know mom it took five years to train a fighting Roman Legion, by then they were so disciplined you could march them over a cliff without a single man breaking rank!"

LENNY - Genuinely amazed.

"You're kidding!"

LUKE – Affirmatively.

"I'm not mom! Every modern Army is based on Roman formations, a company of soldiers is one hundred men, the Romans called it a century, one hundred men..."

LUKE – Pausing as he senses his mother has more on her mind than his passion for all things Roman.

LENNY – Pensively.

"I've got something to tell you Luke, you won't like it, so I'll come right out and say it! Your father wants to take you on a vacation in an RV, you, and him, man-to-man!"

LUKE'S affable smile rapidly diminishes as he scoffs.

"A vacation, in an RV... WITH HIM? You got to be kidding!"

LENNY Tolerantly

"Yes Luke! WITH HIM! He knows he's made mistakes..."

LUKE - Increasingly belligerent as he retorts.

"MISTAKES? Mom, how can you say he makes mistakes when he

ignores us every time his cell phone rings, what about my birthday last year, when he drove off in the middle of my party to do a deal somewhere, did he stop to even consider how dumb I felt in frontof my friends? All that matters to him is profit, I won't go anywhere with him and that's final".

LENNY – Glancing meaningfully around the bedroom.

"He has been... generous!"

LUKE – Contemptuously.

"All this, and a gold Rolex, is not being a father!"

LENNY – Beseechingly.

"Can't you at least meet him halfway?"

LUKE- Obstinately.

"Mom, I'll tell you like it is, I can't conceive anything less appealing than what he calls a man-to-man vacation in an RV!"

LENNY – Sighing heavily.

"OK Luke, he asked me to speak to you and I have, I won't ask you again or try to convince you this vacation would be a chance for both of you to damn well start acting like the father and son you should be!"

LENNY - Walking to the bedroom door, opening it, and pausing to make lingering eye contact with Luke when she adds.

"One day Luke, you'll have children of your own, and like your father, you'll make mistakes, when you do, I hope you get the second chance you won't consider giving your father!"

LENNY- Intentionally not closing the bedroom door, walking briskly to the stairs but stopping half way down when she hears it suddenly slam.

CUT TO - Lenny joins Jeffrey waiting in the hallway. Together they enter the lounge.

LENNY - Wearily settling on one of the white leather settees.

"I could sure use a drink!"

Jeffrey, stepping from behind the bar, clinking ice cubes into two glasses before adding large measures of Courvoisier.

JEFFREY - "I heard some of that! He's not going to move is he!"

LENNY – Surprisingly optimistic.

"He'll go with you Jeff, he doesn't know it himself yet, but he WILL go!"

JEFFREY – Clearly astonished.

"But he just said…?"

LENNY - Knowingly.

"Our son is full of turmoil, but he's not a fool! Only a damn fool hate's forever!"

JEFFREY – Anxiously.

"Can't we get him down here, and talk to him together?"

LENNY – Adamantly.

"Absolutely NO! It must come from him, let him decide in his own time!"

JEFFREY - Settling beside Lenny, placing a large brandy glass in her hand.

LENNY – Decisively.

"When this trip happens, my advice is be patient with him, don't rush things, when he stresses you out, and believe me, he will, prove to him you're not so obsessed with money you can be the father he expects you to be, above all Jeff, I expect you to keep him safe!"

JEFFREY – Reassuringly.

"Len, trust me! Whatever happens, I will keep him safe!"

SCENE FADES…NEW SCENE – SCREEN HEADING…

DOWNTOWN PHEONIX – THREE DAYS LATER

CUT TO - Jeffrey, drawing the Ferrari to a halt beside a military remembrance park showing several highly detailed stone statues of American soldiers in combat situations. When his cell phone suddenly rings he scoops it up, notes the caller is Lenny and makes the connection.

LENNY – Enthusiastically.

"Jeff? Luke's agreed to make the trip!"

LENNY – Repeating when Jeffrey hesitates...

"Did you hear me? Luke's agreed..."

JEFFREY- Unintentionally brusque...

"I heard you, what happened?"

LENNY – Informatively

"I talked to him again! He's not happy, but he *has* agreed to go with you!"

JEFFREY – Advisedly.

"OK! Listen, I'm going to get a cab to follow me home so I can garage my car, then I'll use the cab to go shopping!"

LENNY- Clearly mystified.

"Shopping? For what?"

JEFFREY – Affirmatively.

"For a Recreational Vehicle! See you later!"

SCENE FADES...

NEW SCENE

Visual only...

A CAB ENTERING THE FORCOURT OF A DEALERSHIP FOR RV'S

CUT TO - Jeffrey exits the cab and pays the driver. Immediately he's approached by a balding, overweight salesman whose white shirt show dark stains under both armpits. Following a brief exchange, the salesman makes a sweeping gesture clearly inviting Jeffrey to look around. With a brief glance of obvious indifference to rows of enormous new and used RV's either side of the forecourt Jeffrey wanders over to a collection of smaller older RVs stationed beside the dealership garage. About to dismiss a medium sized RV showing several dents and rusting scars on its hand painted military green bodywork, Jeffrey pauses for a double take when he sees three square plaques bolted to the front fender of the RV. The centre one gives the RV a name - *The Screaming Eagle,* the second shows two names, Hank, and Gus. The third depicts a yellow and white eagle's head being the insignia of 101st Airborne Division. With increasing interest, Jeffrey slides open a wide side door with a large window and climbs inside.

CUT TO – Inside the RV

Jeffrey entering a good-sized central lounge showing a worktop with a sink and a small cooking range powered by a gas bottle located beneath the worktop. One side of the lounge has a four feet seat which is also a storage unit. A triangular corner unit proves to be a WC with a chemical toilet, a wash hand basin but not a shower. Beside the washroom a door leads to a small bedroom showing a wide cupboard at the rear fronted by two sets of top and bottom bunks, the lower ones showing bundles of new bedding wrapped in cellophane. Subdued daylight from a two feet square skylight layered with years of accumulated grime competes with tiny gaps in the curtains of two small portholes beside each of the upper bunks. Returning to the lounge, Jeffrey takes note of two sliding

aluminium doors leading to the cab. In the cab he picks up and reads a sales card resting on the dashboard.

This RV was built by two former servicemen to cover rough terrain. It has four bunks, central locking, a three-litre diesel engine, four-wheel drive, and air-conditioning. Added extras are a pull-out sun canopy and a tubular steel rack above the cab. The rear bedroom has a skylight and a large storage cupboard containing foldaway table and chairs and a portable gas-fired B-B-Q. Other extras are brand-new bedding plus pots, pans, and cutlery.

Our mechanics are confident of its reliability. Price – inclusive of the bodywork being repaired and re-sprayed - $11000.

CUT TO - Jeffrey, stepping down via the side door from the lounge to examine deep treaded steel-reinforced tyres and a circular container at the rear housing a spare wheel.

CUT TO - The salesman, watching Jeffrey from a distance, is confident of a sale as he strides toward him.

CUT TO - JEFFREY – Tersely, before the salesman speaks.

"I like this RV, but not the rust, the lack of a shower, or the price! I don't want it re -sprayed, which will save you money! I'll make one offer payable with an immediate cash transfer via American Express. If we can't do a deal, I'll walk away!"

CUT TO - THE SALESMAN - His smile fading.

"OK, what's your offer?"

JEFFREY – Affirmatively.

"Nine grand, you throw in a full tank of diesel and a new gas bottle!"

THE SALESMAN – Pausing before murmuring.

"Let's go to the office!"

CUT TO – Jeffrey driving the *Screaming Eagle* off the forecourt.

SCENE FADES...

NEW SCENE –

Visual only...

CUT TO - Jeffrey in a hardware store purchasing two boxes of bullets, two six-feet-long fibreglass fishing rods with reels, and a pair of binoculars. Putting everything into the utility cupboard he drives to his next stop.

CUT TO - Jeffrey in a supermarket, loading a shopping cart with several six-packs of beer, a bottle of Jack Daniel's, gallon containers of fruit juice, and tins of Coca-Cola. Other items are a large assortment of tinned food, pre-packed greens and two enormous T-bone steaks.

CUT TO - JEFFREY'S arrival home.

Making a wide turn on the forecourt leaving the RV pointing outward, Jeffrey shuts down the engine and sees Lenny wearing white shorts, flip-flops and a red halter-neck top emerge from the house staring incredulously at the RV.

CUT TO – JEFFREY - Grinning as he climbs down from the cab and places his arm around Lenny's waist.

"Before you say anything, I know it won't ever turn heads, but for what I have in mind it's perfect!"

JEFFREY - Sliding open the side door.

"Come on, I'll show you around!"

As Jeffrey and Lenny enter the RV...

CUT TO - A window overlooking the forecourt where Luke stares contemptuously down at the RV before snatching the curtain closed.

SCENE FADES...

NEW SCENE - MID MORNING THE NEXT DAY.

CUT TO - Jeffrey, wearing trainers, jeans and a t-shirt walking in the searing heat toward the RV carrying a Winchester rifle and a large holdall. Removing keys from his back pocket, two sudden clunks confirm the central locking releasing.

Via the side door, Jeffrey enters the lounge and dropping his holdall onto a lower bunk places the Winchester in the WC. Drawing open the two metal doors he enters the stifling cab, fires up the engine and turns on the air-conditioning.

CUT TO - Lenny, approaching the RV with Luke, carrying a holdall trudging beside her.

CUT TO – LUKE - Brusquely tossing his holdall onto the lounge floor then briefly embracing his mother. Knowing he should close the side door, he ignores it and slumping into the passenger seat sullenly attaches his seat belt. Jeffrey exits the cab, slams the side door closed and gently draws Lenny into his arms.

CUT TO - JEFFREY - The purring engine masking his voice.

"Darling? Don't look so worried! We'll be fine! The longer I go without phoning you, the more everything is going to plan!"

CUT TO - LENNY - Her expression tense as she comments.

"Remember, what I said about being patient!"

CUT TO - JEFFREY - Returning to the cab, attaching his seatbelt, selecting first gear, and mouthing to Lenny.

"I love you! Trust me!"

CUT TO - Lenny, not taking her eyes from the RV until it reaches the end of the drive where the brake lights momentarily glow before it moves out of sight.

CUT TO - Lenny, turning back to the house where she settles on the second step of the mahogany stairway with moistening eyes.

CUT TO – Moments later – A distant view of the house echoing with immensely captivating piano playing.

SCENE FADES...
OPENING SCENE.
THE CAB OF THE RV...

CUT TO – Moving past houses, shops and commercial businesses recede giving way to horizons dominated by vast mountain ranges the only sound amid the silent oppressive atmosphere between father and son is the steady drone of the engine. While Luke stares with simmering hostility straight ahead, Jeffrey, noting how white his knuckles are, constantly relaxes his taut grip on the steering wheel.

CT - JEFFREY – Giving a brief, throat clearing cough.

"It's roughly a hundred and forty miles to Flagstaff Luke, I figure we'll pitch there tonight and head up to the Grand Canyon! What' you reckon?"

CUT TO - LUKE - Glaring cynically at his father, his voice emphatic as he retorts.

"I only agreed to this so-called vacation for mom's sake, now I'm here, I hate everything about it! I want to go home!"

CUT TO - JEFFREY – Imploringly stating.

"Luke, I'm trying to..."

LUKE – Scornfully bellowing.

"I'm not interested in what you're trying to do, I want to go home! I will keep saying it until you turn this rusting heap around and do it!" Instantly releasing his seat belt, Luke draws open both metal doors and retreating to the lounge, noisily crashes them closed. Snatching up his holdall and sitting on the storage seat he removes a sizable laptop and turns it on.

CUT TO - JEFFREY. Slowly shaking his head, glances from his

brilliant white knuckles to a green overhead traffic sign indicating a turnoff for the highway to Flagstaff.

SCENES FADES...

OPENING SCENE

A CAMPSITE IN FLAGSTAFF – LATER THAT DAY...

CUT TO - Jeffrey emerging from a building with sign indicating it's a Campsite Reception Office. Driving to the pitch he's paid for he shuts down the engine and climbs down from the cab. Sliding the side door open he steps into the lounge where Luke, engrossed in fingering the keyboard of his laptop, ignores him.

CUT TO - JEFFREY – Murmuring patiently.

"I'll be in and out setting up the pitch, can you put your feet up?" Without looking at his father, Luke swivels his legs onto the seat. Going to the utility cupboard Jeffrey removes the folding table and chairs and sets them up outside. Reaching up to open the sun canopy proves difficult when two telescopic legs meant to support it drop down indicating the canopy must be supported while putting them in place. Watching his father struggle to finally set the canopy up Luke turns indifferently back to his laptop. Collecting the portable barbie from the bedroom cupboard. Jeffrey ignites it and places the two T-bone steaks onto it and between rotating them sets the table with cutlery, buttered bread and plates filled with pre-wrapped assorted greens.

CUT TO - JEFFREY – Pensively leaning into the lounge.

"Tables laid and chow's ready son!"

LUKE – Curtly militant.

"I'll eat in here!"

Jeffrey patiently nods and places Luke's meal and cutlery on the end of the storage seat. Both meals are consumed in simmering ongoing silence.

NEW SCENE

LATER THAT EVENING.

CUT TO – A small convoy of RVs arriving at the campsite where, not unlike the covered wagons of the old West, they assemble into a huge circle. As sunset approaches billowing smoke carries the appetising aroma of countless Bar-B-Q's.

CUT TO - JEFFREY...

Washing and clearing away the dishes, passing the morose Luke to undo the cellophane wrapped bedding and make up beds on both top bunks. Sitting at the table and pulling the ring on a can of beer, the side door suddenly slams and rebounds slightly open when the catch fails to connect. Listening as Luke climbs to an upper bunk, Jeffrey, opening another beer, sits quietly enjoying as the site winds down amid echoes of receding chatter as families are preparing for bed. Entering the lounge, and by now aware the side door needs to be forcibly slammed for the lock to engage, Jeffrey crashes it closed and locks it. Entering the bedroom to see Luke apparently sound asleep Jeffrey strips down to his boxer shorts and climbs up to the bunk opposite Luke. Switching off the light, nestling under the blankets and squaring the pillow behind his head Jeffrey murmurs.

"Goodnight Luke!"

Predictably, no response comes from Luke...

NEW SCENE
THE FOLLOWING MORNING

CUT TO – JEFFREY - Suddenly awakened by the unmistakable rumble of the side door opening suggesting Luke has left to thumb a ride home. Scrambling into the lounge, with obvious relief Jeffrey sees Luke walking toward the site amenities block carrying a towel and his toiletry bag. Filling the kettle Jeffrey smiles and glances at an unblemished sky confirming the day is set to be a typical Arizona scorcher.

CUT TO - JEFFREY. Sitting under the canopy, sipping coffee as Luke returns.

"I've made fresh coffee! I figure we'll hit the road and have breakfast later!"

CUT TO - LUKE. Moodily silent as he enters the lounge, pours coffee, then sits on the bench to open his laptop. Jeffrey finishes his coffee and begins replacing everything into the RV. A spring-loaded recoiling device on the canopy makes it easier to close than it was to open.

CUT TO - The vacation resumes with Luke in the lounge and Jeffrey glancing at an overhead traffic sign showing they're approaching one of the most iconic tourist destinations in the world. The Grand Canyon National Park.

NEW OPENING SCENE
PARKING LOT - NORTH RIM - THE GRAND CANYON.
EARLY AFTERNOON...

CT – JEFFREY- Drawing to a halt surrounded by cars, luxury air-conditioned coaches, gas-guzzling 4x4s and countless RVs. Shutting down the engine and releasing his seatbelt he gratefully yawns and leans back to stretch his arms. Winding down his window he sees a stand of high fir trees running adjacent to the parking lot for what seems miles. In the distance, nestling between the trees are three buildings constructed to look like pioneering log cabins. One shows an overhead sign stating it's a combined Hotel/Diner. After browsing a colourful brochure that came with the parking fee Jeffrey nudges open the metal doors and enters the lounge to see Luke sat wearing headphones connected to his laptop.

CUT TO - JEFFREY – Politely informative.

"We're here son! The Grand Canyon!"

Getting no reaction whatsoever from Luke Jeffrey gently taps his shoulder and points meaningfully at the headphones. Grudgingly removing them, Luke glares up at his father.

JEFFREY – Repeating.

"We're here Luke, the Grand Canyon! There is a Diner nearby, we could get some breakfast?"

Watching Luke slowly shake his head before replacing the headphones, feeling his patience is on a knife-edge, Jeffrey snatches them clear of Luke's head and tosses them onto his lap.

JEFFREY – Bellowing.

"You know what I'm trying to do here Luke, you don't want any part of it, so what the hell DO you want?"

CUT TO - LUKE – Coldly adamant.

"I want what I asked for yesterday! I'll say the same tomorrow, and the next day! I WANT TO GO HOME...!"

JEFFREY - With seething finality as he turns and strides to the cab.

"YOU WANNA GO HOME! YOU GOT IT!"

CUT TO - JEFFREY - Noisily drawing both doors closed, sagging hot and sweaty into the driving seat, snatching up and connecting his seatbelt, reaching for the ignition key but hesitating then releasing the seat belt and ramming both doors open to re-enter the lounge.

CUT TO - JEFFREY- Aggressively towering over Luke, who's replaced the headphones.

"Is going home what you really want? Can't we at least talk?"

CUT TO - LUKE - Calmly turning off his laptop and placing it beside him on the bench. Removing the headphones he gently sets them down on the laptop. Staring up at his enraged father his china-blue eyes show no sign of fear or intimidation, his voice rock steady when he quietly murmurs.

"I'm your son, I'm fifteen years old, tell me what you think I want to do with my life, tell me what you think my future ambitions are?"

As a sudden heavy silence dominates the lounge, Jeffrey, visibly bewildered, hesitates.

LUKE – Nodding, continues.

"There was a time when I admired how everything you touched made money, then I saw how your obsession for more put me and mom in second place, you could see what you were doing to us, but you did nothing!"

LUKE – Pausing, stating with obvious contempt.

"When mom asked me to come on this so-called vacation, what was man to man about it when you couldn't bring yourself to ask me?"

JEFFREY- Retorting.

"I knew talking to you would get me nowhere!"

LUKE – More contemptuous than ever.

"So let's define things, you knew exactly how I would react to coming on this trip, but you haven't got a clue in hell what my future ambitions are?"

JEFFREY – Aware his wrath is diminishing, murmurs.

"Right at this moment Luke, I can't tell you how sorry I am for not knowing what every father should know, I can only say when I was earning a hundred thousand dollars simply by sending a text or an email I forgot my real wealth was my family. I can only apologize to you, and give you my word, as *one man to another*, never to take you or your mother for granted again!"

As a heavy silence returns, Jeffrey, noting how the pent-up anguish in Luke's eyes distinctly softens, beseechingly adds.

"Your mother said only a damn fool hates forever, I'm not more than you Luke, and you're not less than me. I'm asking for a second chance son?"

When Jeffrey offers his hand, Luke hesitates then slowly accepts it. Briskly returning to the cab, Jeffrey winds up the window and snatches up his cell phone from its charging cradle on the dashboard. Climbing down into the oppressive heat he sees Luke exit from the side door. Forcefully slamming it closed, Jeffrey initiates the central locking and places the keys in the back pocket of his jeans. With silence dividing them father and son walk toward the distant Hotel/Diner.

SCENES FADES...

NEW OPENING SCENE.

CUT TO - Jeffrey and Luke entering a foyer bustling with tourists from all over the world. One side is dominated by a long Reception/Information desk, opposite it is the unrelenting clatter of dishes and voices in a diner. Edging through the crowds to the far end of the foyer they approach a wide stone fireplace showing in its hearth a small mound of smoke-blackened logs, beside the fireplace a pair of wedged open doors lead to a sizable gift shop virtually shoulder to shoulder with tourists. Moving toward beckoning daylight beyond the shop they emerge onto a short-gravelled pathway and walk to a curved stone buttress overlooking the Grand Canyon where, like countless of millions who visit the Canyon, they're instantly captivated by one of the most sublime visual experiences in the world.

Plunging to the mighty Colorado River one mile below and stretching left and right as far as the eye can see a vast panorama of multiple gorges, buttes and plateaus are tinted in a kaleidoscope of indescribable colour randomly broken by the caressing shadow of a passing solitary cloud. Ten thousand centuries in the making, and extending more than two hundred miles, the Canyon ingrains a moment of pause that endures forever...

CUT TO - In the fierce afternoon heat they explore the narrow tourist pathways along the Canyon Rim until...

CUT TO - JEFFREY – Commenting amenably.

"I could sure use a coffee, even better, a king size mixed grill!"

Luke nod's immediate in agreement.

CUT TO - A BOOTH IN THE DINER showing scant conversation between them as they consume the mixed grill.

CUT TO - THE GIFT SHOP - SOMETIME LATER...

Jeffrey buy's a book. Luke buys a crafted Indian bangle.

CUT TO - THEIR RETURN TO THE RV.

When Jeffrey initiates the central locking, to his surprise Luke climbs into the cab.

CUT TO - LUKE – Settling into the passenger seat, murmuring...

"Dad? Why don't we go off road, get away from people?"

Jeffrey, immediately elated, nods, and fires up the engine.

CUT TO - The RV, stopping at a garage in the parking lot to fill the gas tank before heading for the open road.

SCENE FADES...

NEW SCENE - SOMETIME LATER...

CUT TO - The view from the RV's windscreen...Showing desert and distant mountain ranges bordering a highway stretching as straight as an arrow to the horizon where the searing heat creates the illusion the road ascends in hovering tangled confusion.

CUT TO - The steering wheel, confirming how relaxed Jeffrey's become via knuckles that are completely brown.

CUT TO - JEFFREY. Smiling as he glances at Luke.

"So, what *are* your future ambitions Luke?"

LUKE – Amenably turning in his seat to face his father.

"Two things appeal to me dad, one is a career as an Historian!"

JEFFREY- Incredulously.

"Why an Historian?"

LUKE – Amused, but affirmative.

"History fascinates me because we never learn from it!"

JEFFREY – Attentively curious.

"Go on!"

LUKE – Informatively.

"OK, take America for example, we're the richest country in the world, and the most generous, we give billions of dollars to third world countries and do incredible things like putting a man on the moon, yet countless Americans live in dread of illness because they can't afford medical treatment! Where have we progressed?"

JEFFREY- Clearly impressed.

"I sure can't argue with that, what's your second ambition?"

LUKE – Hesitantly.

"My other choice is to write screenplays!"

JEFFREY – Again incredulous.
"SCREENPLAYS? You mean, stories like in the movies?"
LUKE - Grinning...
"Yes dad, exactly like the movies, I told mom about a competition
we're doing in school called 'Movie Idea', it's to see who can write the
best screenplay, the competition is fierce, the school has some brilliant
writers?"
LUKE - hesitates before adding...
"I love movies as an art form, when I picture a scene in my mind's eye I
find it very easy to bring it to life when I write it, a screenplay is like
writing a book, but more complicated..."
JEFFREY – "Why more complicated?"
LUKE – "Because all stories, whether they're action, comedy, romance
or whatever lead to conflict and how that conflict is resolved, in a
screenplay every tiny detail about events and how characters are
reacting is what the writer visualises on a cinema screen!"
JEFFREY- Grinning and somewhat bemused.
"Well I'll be damned, my son the screenwriter!"
LUKE - Curiously.
"I guess you figured I'd want to be a lawyer or a doctor?"
JEFFREY - Shaking his head...
"Hell no, I admire you for knowing what you want to do at such an
early age, I particularly like your definition about history!"
JEFFREY – Pausing, knowingly adding...
"Don't make the mistakes I've made Luke! You only get one life, when
it's over there's no coming back, it's easy to live in a mindset where you
want everything to be permanently ideal, trust me, it's a pipe dream,
count every day, son, and make every day count! You want to raise
pigs, or go prospecting, what can I do to help? You want to write
screenplays, I'm there for you!"
Luke, visibly more contented than he's been in years, casually glances
at the passing terrain and does a rapid double take before pointing and

hollering...
LUKE - "DAD? LOOK!"
JEFFREY- Momentarily startled, sees what Luke is pointing at.
CUT TO - A medium-sized black-and-white mongrel dodging the
carpet of desert foliage while running parallel with the RV. When
Jeffrey pulls off the road and the dog veers toward the RV, Luke
quickly enters the lounge and approaches the side door..
JEFFREY – Following him, shouting...
"Not yet Luke, lets watch him first, and check him out!"
CUT TO - Father and son staring down from the window in the
sliding door to see the dog panting as it frantically looks for an
opening into the RV. With no collar, undoubtedly starving, but
showing no sign of foaming at the mouth or aggression, Jeffrey gives
Luke a slight nudge.
JEFFREY - "He looks okay! Let him in!"
The instant Luke slides the door open the dog scrambles into the
lounge and with obvious excitement runs straight toward him.
LUKE – Leaning down and calming the dog by tousling its ears.
"Where have you come from little fella?"
JEFFREY – Tersely, as he watches the dog's response to Luke.
"I reckon some son of a bitch drove off and abandoned him!"
JEFFREY - Grinning as he murmurs.
"He sure looks hungry, what have we got to feed him with?"
Luke immediately opens the fridge and removes a tinfoil packet of
chicken slices the dog begins to devour as fast as he pulls them from
the wrapping. Jeffrey opens a tin of corned beef and forking it onto a
galvanized plate, hands it to Luke. In seconds, the dog ravenously
consumes it. The next item the fridge provides is a plastic bottle of
chilled water, the inevitable crackling sound as Luke pours it onto the
plate is in perfect unison with the dog's desperate lapping.
JEFFREY – Glancing from the dog to Luke, conveying he knows
exactly what's coming.

LUKE - Gazing beseechingly at his father'

"Dad, can I keep him?"

JEFFREY - Contemplating the emptiness of the surrounding terrain.

"You want him son, you got him. Let's get back on the road!"

When Jeffrey attempts to close the door the catch refuses to engage until he slides it wide open and forcefully slams it.

SCENE FADES...

NEW OPENING SCENE – THE CAB.

CUT TO - The exhausted dog, settling at Luke's feet where it promptly falls asleep.

JEFFREY - With obvious amusement.

"You got yourself a dog son, what' you gonna call him?"

LUKE - Exclaiming with boyish delight.

"Beric! I'm going to call him Beric!"

JEFFREY – Perplexed.

"BERIC? What kind of a name is Beric?"

LUKE - Grinning as he stretches down to smooth the slumbering dog.

"I watched an old movie last week, *Knights of the Round Table,* with Robert Taylor, there's a scene where he comments how much he loves his horse, which saves his life when it pulls him out of quicksand, the horse's name was Beric!"

JEFFREY – Drawling tongue in cheek...

"Ah yes, Beric, I always did like that name!"

As the cab fill with laughter...

CUT TO - THE WINDSCREEN and a large sign beside the highway stating.

Campsite – Two miles ahead.

Trailers and RV's welcome.

Clean amenities – Provisions – Antique shop.

Clem Hudson – Prop

JEFFREY – Suggesting.

"What do you think about pitching here tonight? We can freshen up, get our bearings, and figure where to go next!"

LUKE - Instantly agreeable.

"Anything you say Dad!"

CUT TO - Jeffrey drives into the campsite and halts outside a large wooden cabin fronted by a wide front veranda and an overhanging roof providing shade from the intense sunlight. A sign nailed to the roof support states - *'Book in here.'*

CUT TO - A man in his early sixties sat beside a small table on the veranda looks up from a paperback he's reading. Wearing shorts, a green T-shirt and moccasins, the sides of his long-faded military forage cap show a hint of snow-white hair that contrasts with a face the colour of stained mahogany. Watching Jeffrey shut down the engine and climb down, the man folds back a page in the book and drops it on the table. Curiously surveying the RV from end to end he walks toward Jeffrey.

CUT TO - THE MAN - Extending his hand.

"Howdy, I'm Clem Hudson, the owner!"

JEFFREY – Noting both Clems iron grip and aura of unmissable toughness.

"Hi! My name is Jeffrey Blake. The boy in the RV is my son Luke. We'd like a pitch for the night. We also have a dog!"

CLEM – Acknowledging Luke with a brief wave.

"No sweat! Let's get you booked in!"

Jeffrey follows Clem across the veranda to a compact office.

CUT TO - THE OFFICE. Showing a small service counter, a few chairs, an ageing box-shaped television, and an upright glass-fronted refrigerator filled with soft drinks and bottled water. A notice on a nearby wall curtly states.

Camp Rules

No swearing - Keep the noise down.

Dogs on a lead always – otherwise secured to vehicles.

CUT TO - CLEM – Amenably, as he steps behind the counter and nods toward the fridge.

"Help yourself to a cold drink!"

CUT TO – JEFFREY – Smiling as he declines the drink. Not failing to see when Clem leans forward to fill in a site admission form the peak of his forage cap shows the oval shaped parachute insignia of American Airborne Forces and the legendary letters 'USMC'.

CLEM – Seeing Jeffrey remove his wallet.

"Square me up when you leave!"

CLEM - Not missing Jeffrey's noticeable surprise.

"I don't get any trouble here, if I do, I handle it! The showers and washroom are in the centre of the site, there's a store if you need to stock up on anything, and an antique shop that might interest you!"

JEFFREY - Gesturing to Clem's forage cap...

"You were in the Marines Clem?"

CLEM - Drawling informatively.

"Yeah! I did two tours in Nam with a Reconnaissance Team!"

CLEM - Nodding toward the door, inquiring.

"That rig you're driving, where did you get it?"

JEFFREY – Informatively.

"From a dealer in Phoenix! Why do you ask Clem?"

CLEM – Knowingly.

"Because I'd know it anywhere, it's the '*Screaming Eagle!* I knew the guys who built it, Hank Prichard and Gus Austin, ex-paras from

101st.!Whatever you paid for it, you got yourself a hell of wagon!"

JEFFREY - Clearly warming to Clem.

"It was the names, and the airborne insignia that made me look at it, then buy it!"

CLEM – With obvious remorse.

"They're both dead! Cancer got Hank! Gus had a massive heart attack!"

CLEM – Pausing before reflectively adding.

"They were both in Nam, they had a real bad time in the A Shau

Valley, when they left the service they found that RV in a scrapyard and with useful contacts in a military supply depot got everything they needed to rebuild it, including a new engine and tyres, the only paint they could get was military combat green, they drifted around the State doing odd jobs and getting into pub brawls, they sure broke a few heads, they usually finished up here, never paid for their pitch, but were great to have a few beers with and swap yarns.

JEFFREY - Nodding appreciatively.

"You've cleared up my curiosity about the RV!"

JEFFREY – On an impulse.

"Things haven't been too good with me and my son lately, I want to take him somewhere off road where we can spend time together, do you know anywhere hereabouts we could go?"

CLEM – Thoughtfully hesitant.

"Well...there's a small lake in the mountains near here called Prairie Basin, it's isolated, the swimming and the fishing's good, but the trail leading to it is as hairy as hell, it would challenge a tank!"

JEFFREY – Undeterred.

"Would my rig handle the trail Clem?"

CLEM- Scoffing.

"Hell yes, the other thing about going up there is the weather, a dense mist, where you wouldn't see a hand in front of you, can drop down in seconds!"

CLEM – Meaningfully.

"It sure ain't the place to be if anything goes wrong!"

JEFFREY – Aware what Clem is inferring.

"Clem, I'm a businessman, I've never been in any of the services, but I

hail from excellent military stock, my grandfather was in the 101st when he was killed in Bastogne!"

CLEM – Pausing, but clearly impressed.

"OK, when you leave, turn right, two miles down the road you'll see a scrub track resembling a long scar across the desert, it'll lead you to an opening in the mountains which is the trail up to the lake, the trail is not man made, it's a natural a ledge wide enough for your rig, take it dead slow, when you reach the top you'll see a fork leading left and right, take the left one which winds for half a klick to the lake, on no account turn right, it leads further into the mountains to the butt end of nowhere!"

CLEM – Informatively adding...

"The views up there will blow you away, but under no circumstances attempt to second guess the weather, if you decide to come back down but see the light fading, stay put and wait for bright clear sky!"

JEFFREY – Nodding, memorizing every detail.

"Got you Clem!"

CUT TO – (Audible) - The distance sound of an approaching vehicle.

CLEM – Handing Jeffrey a long length of nylon rope.

"Duty calls, pitch wherever you like, any problems gimme a shout! Secure your dog to your fender and don't piss me off by not cleaning up after him, return the rope when you leave!"

CUT TO – Jeffrey and Clem leaving the office. Clem walks over to the newcomer.

CUT TO - JEFFREY – Grinning as he climbs into cab exclaiming.

"You said you wanted to go off road, the guy who owns this site told me about a secluded lake with good swimming and fishing."

LUKE – Immensely curious.

"Where Dad?"

JEFFREY – Firing up the engine.

"It's up in the mountains near here, it sounds perfect for us, I'll tell you all about it while we're setting up our pitch!"

SCENE FADES...

NEW OPENING SCENE – EARLY EVENING

CUT TO - Jeffrey and Luke entering Clem's campsite shop conveying mutual surprise at the range of goods available. Items they purchase are a dog collar and a lead, boxes of tinned dog food, two large stainless-steel bowls, loaves of bread, numerous packages of frozen bacon and sausages plus matches and a box of candles.

CUT TO – Entering Clem's antique shop they see goods ranging from ornamental trivia to antique guns and swords. Of immediate interest to Luke is an assortment of knives and bayonets stabbed into a log for display. One of them is an iconic Fairbairn Sykes dagger issued to the British special forces in World War two. Making the weapon even more unique is a miniature insignia of the Parachute Regiment at the base of the hilt. Locating its well-worn leather sheath Luke loses no time buying it.

CUT TO – Their return to the RV where a highly animated Beric welcomes them the instant they slide the side door open. Storing away their provisions they sit talking beneath the canopy until encroaching darkness and a sudden chill in the air hint at bedtime. After Luke makes cocoa and Jeffrey slams the side door closed they climb to their upper bunks smiling down at Beric when he settles between the lower bunks. Bidding each other good night, the bedroom plunges into darkness.

SCENE FADES...

NEW OPENING SCENE – THE NEXT MORNING.

CUT TO – Jeffrey drawing the RV to a halt outside Clem's cabin. Leaving the engine running when he sees Clem emerge from the office, he climbs down to pay him.

CUT TO - CLEM – Vaguely smiling as he puts the site fee into a pocket in his shorts.

"Still going up to the Basin?"

JEFFREY - Affirmatively...

"Yep!"

CLEM – Amiably.

"Anything you're not clear about?"

JEFFREY – Extending his hand.

"We'll be fine Clem!"

CLEM - Murmuring advisedly.

"Keep in mind what I said about the weather up there! Don't take any chances!"

JEFFREY – Confidently.

"Will do Clem! Thanks for your help, we'll look in on you when we come back!"

Returning to the cab Jeffrey and Luke wave to Clem as they move off.

CUT TO – The Veranda

Staring at the departing RV as it pulls onto the highway and turns right, Clem briefly shrugs before sitting beside the table. Opening his book and locating the latest bent back page he settles back to begin reading.

SCENE FADES...

NEW OPENING SCENE.

CUT TO - Minutes later, Jeffrey turns onto the scrub track stretching across the open desert.

CUT TO - The rear of the *Screaming Eagle* obscured by the dust it throws up heading toward a distant mountain range and the trail to Prairie Basin.

SCENE FADES...

NEW OPENING SCENE

CUT TO – The view from the RV's windscreen showing a gap in the mountain range leading to a narrow gorge bordered by towering walls. Moments after entering the gorge Jeffrey drives onto the extreme incline of the natural ledge. Moving at little more than walking pace the *Screaming Eagle* shows no strain whatsoever as its powerful engine and deeply treaded tyres effortlessly consume the rugged uneven surface. The scenery is breath-taking. The sheer drops beside the ledge as they climb higher give huge emphasis to what Clem said about moving in anything less than bright clear daylight.

CUT TO - JEFFREY - Apprehensively glancing down from his cab window.

"A bit hairy Luke! I'll be glad to get to the top!"
LUKE – Nodding, engrossed in the dramatic surroundings with Beric cradled on his lap vigilantly surveying the road ahead. Minutes later, they reach the summit and see the fork Clem mentioned.
LUKE - "Which way Dad?"
JEFFREY - Knowingly.
"Left son, definitely left!"
CUT TO - The windscreen showing a series of curving bends which broaden revealing a wide area dropping down to a small lake surrounded by dense fir trees.
JEFFREY – Halting twenty feet from the lake and shutting down the engine. When all three exit to the absolute silence of their idyllic surroundings, as father and son glance at each other with broad contented grins Beric breaks the silence when he plods over to the lake to eagerly drink. Jeffrey, hot and sweaty, begins stripping to his boxer shorts then strides toward the lake.
JEFFREY- Shouting exuberantly.
"Last one in does the washing-up!"
LUKE - Grinning as Jeffrey plunges into the lake, quickly strips down to chase after him. Beric hesitates before joining them. Following the spontaneous cooldown they erect the sun canopy for welcome shade and place the table and chairs beneath it.
JEFFREY - Emerging from the RV drawing Luke's razor-sharp commando dagger from its sheath then firmly standing on the waist of his expensive designer jeans to tautly stretch a leg upward and sever it just below the crouch. Doing the same with the remaining leg Jeffrey pulls on a homemade pair of shorts complete with dangling shards of cotton.
CUT TO - Luke - Promptly cannibalising his own jeans.
Removing the six-feet-long fibreglass fishing rods from the bedroom utility cupboard and baiting the hooks with bread, they holler with delight when the highly flexible tips begin jerking towards the water.

In the fierce unrelenting heat, they constantly enter the lake to cool down and layer each other with high protection sunscreen. Lounging beneath the canopy, while Jeffrey reads the book he bought at the Grand Canyon Luke fingers his keyboard working on his screenplay. Laying in the shade beneath the RV, Beric is never less than watchful and alert.

CUT TO – THEIR FIRST SUNSET.

Cooking the fish they caught on the barbie man and boy are compelled to pause and stare at the horizon where the sun, a massive slowly descending orange ball seems close enough to lean forward and touch.

LUKE – Staring in awe, murmuring.

"It's almost as if God is turning down a dimmer switch on another day!"

Jeffrey grins and nods.

CUT TO - THE LAKE AREA NOW IN COMPLETE DARKNESS.

Sitting in abject silence and drawn to billions of twinkling stars and those that shoot across the heavens before burning out, when the crisp evening air changes to the usual cold chill they enter the RV and close the side door with its unavoidable slam. No longer on a campsite they feel akin to two boys who've made themselves a den in the wilds as the RV seems to wrap itself protectively around them. Luke connects a long lead from a cigarette outlet in the cab to his laptop so they can watch movies on his laptop, the first being '*Psycho*' famous for a good story and <u>sound effects regarded by many as the most terrifying in cinema history.</u>

So passes their first day at Prairie Basin.

SCENE FADES...

NEW OPENING SCENES...

The following two weeks are shown via brief scenarios...

Between countless cooldowns Jeffrey teaches Luke to shoot the first

American semi-automatic weapon, the iconic Winchester Rifle. Luke proves to be more interested in how its underlever action feeds bullets into the breach than firing it.

Beric, their all-round radar, suddenly growls and rigidly stares at the fir trees at the far side of the lake where father and son see a small Bambi like Elk emerge to approach the water and drink. Snatching up the Winchester Jeffrey takes aim but fleeting eye contact with Luke's raised eyebrows is all it takes for him to lower it. Bambi drinks and returns to the forest.

By now deeply suntanned, and bonding closer by the day, father and son share hilarious moments such as bean fights, flicking baked beans at each other from the edge of their forks. Luke proves to be a natural mimic with his over the-top impressions of famous actors, his most impressive being his John Wayne drawl.

Playing chess and poker beneath the canopy is a time-consuming welcome pastime.

CUT TO - **FIRST ACTION SCENE...**

CUT TO – Father and son wearing trainers, home-made shorts and white vests are returning to the lake from what they call their safari, their exploration of their surroundings. Walking side by side along a narrow trail leading back to the lake, with one hand on the barrel and the other on the stock Jeffrey carries the Winchester behind his neck. Approaching a bend in the trail with Beric out of sight as he forages ahead when they suddenly hear his continuous growling Jeffrey swings down the Winchester and levers a round into the breech.

JEFFREY - Cautiously abrupt.

"Luke? Call him back!"

LUKE – Shouting...

"BERIC! COME HERE BOY!"

Beric returns to Luke's side, staring at the bend but still growling.

JEFFREY - Glancing anxiously in all directions.

"What the hell's bugging him?"

LUKE - Pensively...

"He's warning us about something the other side of this bend!"
Cautiously walking around the bend father and son are horrified to see
in the distance a coiled up Western Diamondback Rattlesnake, its
bony tail making the chilling rattle guaranteed to terrify the bravest of
men.

JEFFREY - Instantly hoisting the Winchester into his shoulder, taking
aim, leaning into the weapon for stability, gently squeezing the trigger,
reloading and firing again even as the first thunderous retort shatters
the silence.

CUT TO - The snake, briefly pivoting upward before dropping down
motionless.

JEFFREY – With obvious panic dominating his voice.

"Luke? Don't move! Don't let Beric follow me!"

CUT TO – LUKE - Grasping Beric's collar, watching Jeffrey
cautiously approach the snake while aiming the Winchester directly at
it.

CUT TO – THE SNAKE - Its head disintegrated.

JEFFREY - Lowering the Winchester, signalling Luke to join him.

LUKE - Continuing to restrain Beric as he approaches and stares with
a mammoth shiver of revulsion at the snake.

JEFFREY – Clearly un-nerved as he makes fearful eye contact with
Luke before nodding toward Beric.

"If he hadn't warned us, we would have walked straight into this snake,
and anything might have happened, Luke, we need to get off this
mountain, I don't mean tomorrow, I mean right now!"

LUKE – Nodding, not about to clash with his father's obvious fear.

"You said it dad, let's get the hell out of here!"

CUT TO - The easy-going tranquillity of the last two weeks changing
to oppressive silence as they walk back to the lake scouring the ground
ahead with vigilance equal to Beric.

CUT TO – THEIR ARRIVAL AT THE LAKE.

JEFFREY- Very affirmatively.

"No last swims, or coffee Luke, I want to get moving!"

CUT TO – Father and son animatedly breaking camp. The last item to go on the RV is the Winchester when Jeffrey places it in the WC.

CUT TO - JEFFREY - Gazing from the sky showing diminishing daylight, then to Luke.

JEFFREY – Informatively

"We had a great time here Luke, I'll never forget it, but after what just happened I can't wait to get off this mountain, I figure in less than half an hour we'll be safely crossing the track to the highway, we'll stay at Clem's place tonight, and make an early start for home tomorrow!"

JEFFREY – Hesitating before adding.

"When Clem told me about this lake I was so determined to bring you here I didn't give a thought about snakes, if I had, I wouldn't have come near it!"

JEFFREY – Pensively explaining.

"When I was a small boy my mother took me to Chicago to visit her sister, we went for a walk on a pier and stopped to talk to an old guy who was fishing, when he removed the lid from a bucket half full of long squirming worms I was so revolted I dropped the toy I was carrying into the bucket, the old guy shook the worms off it and handed it to me, but by then I was hiding behind my mother so he gave it to her, when we left the pier, I snatched it from her hand and tossed it into the sea, I've had an ingrained fear of snakes ever since!"

LUKE – Understandingly.

"Thanks for telling me the story dad, it explains a lot!"

JEFFREY - Affirmatively.

"Not a word about that snake to your mother, it will only get her all riled up!"

LUKE - Emphatically.

"Dad, trust me! It never happened!"

JEFFREY – Again glancing at the darkening sky.

"Come 'on son, let's get the hell out of here!"
CUT TO - When all three enter the RV, as though locking out the wilderness itself Jeffrey vigorously slams the side door closed. Settling into their seats with Beric on the floor he turns the ignition key only to hear the labouring drone of a flat battery. Glancing despairingly at Luke and trying again, although the engine grudgingly fires up Jeffrey's increasing agitation is palpable in the way he noisily revs the engine to restore power to the battery.
JEFFREY – As the noise of the revving recedes.
"Watching those movies drained the battery, why the hell didn't I think to run the engine every day to keep it charged?"
LUKE – Keenly observing his father's anguish, but not commenting.
CUT TO - The RV - Pulling away from the lake.
CUT TO – SEVERAL MINUTES LATER.
JEFFREY- Suddenly slamming on the brakes, instantly grinding the RV to a halt before he bangs the steering wheel with both fists furiously bellowing.
"SONOFABITCH! DAMN IT! DAMN IT TO HELL!"
LUKE - Staring in bewilderment at his father.
"Dad, what's wrong?"
JEFFREY – Massively enraged.
"By now we should have turned to get on the trail down the mountain, but I've driven past it, we're headed further into the mountains!"
LUKE – Calmly stating.
"Wow Dad when you shouted I thought it was something serious, all we need to do is reverse back to the turnoff?"
JEFFREY - Slowly shaking his head, again glancing at the darkening sky.
"I'll drive further on and find somewhere to turn around, it'll be a lot easier than reversing!"
Moments after Jeffrey begins driving, like a blanket dropped over a flashlight any view of the trail ahead instantly vanishes when the mist

Clem warned him about rapidly descends. In the split second he takes to again slam on the brakes any hope of finding somewhere to turn is shrouded by dense impenetrable grey mist.
CUT TO - JEFFREY - Gazing at the murky grey wall now dominating the cab. Revving the engine again to boost the battery he turns off the ignition and pulls out the keys.
JEFFREY – Dejectedly in the sudden silence.
"We're grounded, we can't move until this clears, probably not until the morning, dammit, the last thing I wanted was another night on this mountain?"
CUT TO - THE LOUNGE.
When all three enter the lounge, Jeffrey settles on the bench, welcoming Beric who jumps up and sits beside him.
JEFFREY – Curtly affirmative.
"It's going to be a long night, I don't trust the battery, so no movies unless there's power in your laptop, and no internal lights, when it gets dark, we'll use candles!"
LUKE - Agreeably.
"There's always chess dad?"
JEFFREY- His tense grimace momentarily relaxing.
"OK, chess it is!"
CUT TO - THE LOUNGE – SOMETIME LATER...
With encroaching darkness and no sign of the mist clearing the lounge is illuminated by candles as father and son become engrossed in games of chess. Between games, Luke makes cups of Cocoa, and sandwiches grossly overfilled with cheese and mayonnaise.
CUT TO- JEFFREY -Stretching his arms up as he draws a deep yawn.
LUKE – Also yawning as he checkmates Jeffrey.
"I was thinking dad, instead of ringing Mom to tell her we're on our way home, why don't we just turn up and surprise her?"
JEFFREY – Encouragingly.
"Better still, why don't you call her when we're a mile from the house

and tell her we're still a hundred miles away?"
LUKE – Enthusiastically.
"Dad! That's brill!"
CUT TO - THE BEDROOM.
In the flickering candlelight Luke strips down to his shorts and climbs
up to his bunk.
CUT TO – THE LOUNGE – Where Jeffrey closes both metal doors
to the cab and blows out the candles. Undressing and dropping his
clothes on the lower bunk, he hears Beric settle between the lower
bunks and climbs to his bed.
JEFFREY - Reassuringly as he settles in his bunk.
"In the morning I'll reverse back to the turnoff, we'll be on off this
mountains before we know it!"
LUKE - Murmuring in the darkness.
"I can't wait to see Mom!"
JEFFREY - For altogether different reasons.
"Neither can I son, neither can I!"
LUKE - "It's been a terrific vacation!"
JEFFREY – I can't tell you how much it's meant to me or how proud I
am of you!"
LUKE - Mumbling sleepily...
"Goodnight Dad."
JEFFREY – Contently.
"Goodnight Son!"
Beyond the snug security of the 'Screaming Eagle', the pleasant aroma
of blown out candles and Cocoa enticing man and boy to sleep, the
only sound to challenge the dense mist and the absolute silence is an
occasional ping from the engine as it contracts and cools off...
SCENE FADES
ENDING THREE WEEK FLASHBACK...
CUT TO - OPENING SCENES...
As father and son continue to stare in rigid abject terror at the

rattlesnake between the lower bunks it suddenly uncoils and slithers into a dark narrow recess beneath Luke's lower bunk. Glistening with sweat and dominated by more terror than he's ever known, Jeffrey is incapable of anything other than to gaze in statue like dread at the point where the snake moved out of sight. When a desperate boyish yelp draws his gaze to Luke's near naked vulnerability, rather than terror Jeffrey is consumed by the protective instinct any parent feels when they see their young in danger. Glancing into the lounge to see the remaining two reptiles not approaching the bedroom Jeffrey leans pensively out from his bunk and pushes the door firmly closed. Snatching up a pillow to soak up blinding rivulets of sweat streaming into his eyes, he discards the pillow, eases his bedding aside and continually watching for movement from the lower recess cautiously moves along his bunk to slide open the nearest door and grasp the small steel eyelet of one of the fibre glass fishing rods. Carefully hoisting it up to his bunk he reverses it and after lowering the tip to the floor ejects globules of sweat in all directions as he vigorously shakes his head.

JEFFREY – Shouting with mammoth emphasis.

"LUKE? DON'T MOVE! DON'T DO ANYTHING...!"

Bending the highly flexible rod into the recess, Jeffrey aggressively moves it from side to side until the snake, rattling furiously, emerges between the bunks to become a lethal defensive coil. Constantly blinking to clear ever increasing sweat from his eyes Jeffrey raises the rod until it briefly contacts with the ceiling and with all the force he can muster begins relentlessly pounding the reptile until it attempts to rear up only for the steel eyelet to strike it squarely between its eyes instantly killing it. In the silence as the rattles diminish Jeffrey, saturated and trembling, watches the coil slowly unravel then uses the rod to laboriously nudge the hideous remains back into the recess. Setting the rod aside, he quickly climbs up to sit beside a severely traumatised Luke.

JEFFREY – Gently drawing Luke into his arms.

"I got you Luke! It's OK! I got you... I got you!"

Continuing to hold Luke and gazing despairingly around the bedroom Jeffrey pauses to stare up at the grime layered skylight in the ceiling.

LUKE - Mumbling with intense remorse.

"Dad! I killed Beric! All this is my fault!"

JEFFREY – Easing himself away from Luke.

"What do you mean? YOUR fault?"

LUKE - Definitively.

"Beric woke me up in the middle of the night, everything was black, I opened the door half way to let him out, but when the mist came in he growled and wouldn't go outside, I was shivering, I knew if I pulled the door wide open to slam it you would be angry with me for startling you so I closed it as far as it would go and went back to my bunk!"

JEFFREY - His slow nod confirming he understands everything Luke is saying.

LUKE - Pausing to shudder before continuing.

"When Beric woke me up, scratching the bedroom door as if he desperately needed to relieve himself, I opened it!"

JEFFREY - Booming incredulously...

"YOU WENT INTO THE LOUNGE...?"

LUKE – Retorting.

"No, when I opened the door, everything happened so fast, I only saw the snakes when Beric brushed past me and charged at them, he didn't stand a chance against them when they reared up at him!"

LUKE - Staring down at his hands, tensely wringing one against the other.

"I was absolutely terrified, I knew I couldn't save him, I slammed the door so hard it rebounded open as I ran to my bunk!"

With his strained expression conveying the unimaginable if Luke had tried to rescue his dog, Jeffrey climbs down from the bunk and facing Luke grips his wrists with a sharp attention-grabbing tug.

JEFFREY – Very forcefully stating.

"Stop right there Luke, listen to what I'm saying and get it into your head, YOU didn't kill Beric, and you didn't get us into this horrifying situation, Clem warned me about the weather up here but even though I saw it changing all I could think about was getting us off this damn mountain!"

JEFFREY – Releasing Luke wrists before continuing.

"I know how much you loved Beric, more so because he undoubtedly saved your life, I can't imagine how you're feeling right now, but none of this is your fault, my fear and my panic got us into this god-awful mess.

LUKE – Gazing directly at Jeffrey.

"Is that what you really think Dad?"

JEFFREY- Definitely.

"It's not what I think, it's what I know, we'll get you another dog if that's what you want, but we need to both get dressed and talk about how we're getting out of this hellhole!"

CUT TO - JEFFREY – Pulling on his shorts, feeling for a slight bulge in a back pocket before putting on his T-shirt and trainers.

CUT TO - LUKE – Suddenly giving fearsome whimper when he draws back a curtain in the side window to look outside.

JEFFREY – Immediately climbing up beside to Luke but recoiling after drawing open the curtain.

CUT TO - EXTERIOR OVERHEAD SCENE SHOWING...

The entire area surrounding the RV layered with a virtual carpet of rattlesnakes.

LUKE - Anxiously watching Jeffrey step down from the bunk.

"DAD? Where are they all coming from?"

JEFFREY - Passing the back of his hand across his sodden forehead.

"I don't know Luke, I just don't know, of all the places we might have stopped in that mist, we had to stop here!"

Jeffrey walks to the bedroom door and easing it open no more than half an inch, peers into the lounge.

CUT TO - THE LOUNGE – Showing Beric's remains, and more reptiles.

JEFFREY - Securing the door, then using a pillowcase to meticulously clean the rod he used to kill the snake.

JEFFREY – Tensely informative while staring meaningfully at Luke.

"The lounge is like a scene from hell, but luckily I closed both doors to the cab?"

LUKE – Fearfully.

"What are you saying dad?"

JEFFREY – Affirmatively.

"I've been thinking about where things stand, there's only one way we're getting out of this and that's to get over to the cab, with both lounge doors firmly closed, there can't possibly be any snakes in there!"

JEFFREY – Pausing before continuing.

"I'll open the skylight and crawl over to the cab, I'll climb down into it then reverse back to the trail down the mountain!"

LUKE – Glancing incredulously at the skylight.

"How can you do that, you always lock the cab doors?"

JEFFREY – Informatively.

"I always put ignition keys in my back pocket, I can open them using the central locking!"

LUKE – Shaking his head with fearful increasing scepticism.

"Dad, what if something goes wrong?"

JEFFREY - "Like what?"

LUKE – Logically.

"Like falling off the roof! Don't do this dad, don't do it, you've seen what's out there!"

JEFFREY – Raising a hand to stem Luke's growing hysteria.

"LUKE? CALM DOWN AND LISTEN TO ME! We know the cab is safe, I can easily get to it via the roof, it's the only chance we've got!"

LUKE - Grasping at straws...

"Well..., we could wait? Maybe someone will come and..."
JEFFREY – With increasing exasperation.
"For God's sake Luke, we've been in these mountains for two weeks
and haven't seen another living soul, if anyone did come up here,
they'd head straight to the lake and it's at least a mile away, the chances
of someone finding us are a million to one and damn well non-
existent!"
LUKE - With beseeching reasoning.
"DAD! Sooner or later mom will get concerned about us, she'll get a
whole army looking for us!"
JEFFREY - Dismissively.
"OK, but how long before she gets worried enough to start looking for
us, she has no idea where we are, and Arizona's a mighty big place!"
LUKE - Persistently...
"Well..., maybe Clem will come up to look for us?"
JEFFREY – Incensed.
"We can't wait to see what Clem might do or not do, he could well
figure we came down the mountain and headed straight for home!"
JEFFREY – Pausing, sighing heavily with increasing stress.
"God knows you've seen enough horror since we woke up, I don't want
to frighten you, but you've got to know how desperate things are, that
we survived a rattler getting in here is a miracle, but we're stranded out
here with no chance whatsoever of being found, both cell phones in
the cab so we have no way of calling for help, in terms of weapons, all
we've got are the fishing rods and that military dagger of yours!"
JEFFREY – Hesitating, before ominously continuing.
"We haven't got any water and we're sweating huge amounts of fluid
we can't replace, by midday this bedroom will be an oven, if we wait
for your mother, or Clem, we'll be so dehydrated we won't be able to
do anything, the bottom line is, we can't depend on anyone except
each other, surely you can see that?"
JEFFREY - Seeing Luke's eyes glaze over.

"Come down here son."

When Luke, shivering with dread climbs down, Jeffrey hauls him into a tight embrace before firmly extending him to arm's length.

JEFFREY - Compellingly.

"You know how terrified I am of snakes, but I've got to overcome it, getting to the cab is the only possible way out of this, I need you to be strong Luke, you've got to trust me!"

JEFFREY – Reassuringly'

Imagine we're back home on the forecourt, don't you think I couldn't cross the roof and get into the cab without falling, I won't make a move out there I don't stop to carefully consider, with any luck, in a few minutes from now I'll be reversing back to the turnoff!"

LUKE - Passing the back of his hand over his eyes before nodding grudging consent.

JEFFREY – "Good man!"

Releasing Luke, Jeffrey straddles both lower bunks and draws back a bolt on the skylight, a slight creak as he opens it no more than two inches allows a welcome surge of fresh air into the bedroom.

CUT TO - THE ROOF - Stretching to the luggage rack posing no danger.

JEFFREY - Climbing down.

"There's nothing up there except the rack above the cab!"

LUKE – Murmuring advisedly.

"DAD?"

JEFFREY – Massively uptight as he retorts.

"What Luke, what is it now?"

LUKE- Pensively.

"I was only going to suggest the roof will be hot, we should do something to protect your hands and knees, you should take one of the fishing rods, just in case?"

JEFFREY – Nodding.

"Good thinking son, we'll do something with strips of bed sheets, meanwhile, get dressed!"

While Luke obediently begins dressing, Jeffrey locates his commando dagger and after cutting a bed sheet into long strips, wedges the dagger firmly into the gap beneath the door.

JEFFREY – Pointing to the dagger as Luke helps bind his hands and knees.

"That's to stop any chance of the door opening when we are on the move! When you hear me start the engine, get onto your bunk, and stay there, I'll reverse back to the turnoff and head down the mountain, when we reach the highway, I'll call 911 and get some expert help!"

LUKE - Emotionally...

"Dad! Please be careful out there!"

JEFFREY – Raw emotion constricting his voice.

"As terrifying as this is, we will get out of it, when we do, I swear to God, we will never lose each other again!"

After clinging to each other for several tense moments, Jeffrey, straddling both lower bunks, pushes the skylight wide open until it lays flat on the roof. Hauling himself outside with his feet dangling in the bedroom, as Luke passes up a fishing rod, Jeffrey forces a grim smile saying...

"When you see me climb down into the cab, do exactly what I said!"

JEFFREY – Without another word, beginning the crawl toward the cab..

LUKE – Straddling the lower bunks, fearfully watching his father's every move...

SCENE FADES...

NEW SCENE

CUT TO - THE ROOF OF THE RV.

A brief overhead view shows Jeffrey cautiously moving toward the cab, it also depicts the horrendous infestation surrounding the RV at ground level.

JEFFREY - His thinking relayed in AUDIBLE voiceover.
"The roof is unbearably hot! Thank God Luke thought about protecting my hands and knees! I've got to get him home, I promised Lenny I'd keep him safe! I've never been more afraid! I feel I'm on plank above a snake pit! I won't look down! Whatever happens I won't look down!"
CUT TO - Moments later...
With all his weight behind it, Jeffrey places a knee onto a projecting rivet that penetrates the binding causing a brief surge of brief pain and a downward glance.
JEFFREY – Massively unnerved as he reaches the roof rack to see it's made with stainless steel and rigidly bolted to the roof. Firmly grasping it, he leans out to stare down at the cab door handle.
JEFFREY- VOICEOVER...
"The handle to the cab door is within reach, gripping the roof rack, I can easily swing down into the cab and slam the door! We'll soon be on the move!"
Placing the fishing rod astride the roof rack Jeffrey quickly unwinds the strip of blanket protecting his hand and reaches into his back pocket for the keys to find they're snagged on a strand of tough cotton, impatiently jerking them free, they slip from his sodden hand and slide across the roof where they only stop when they collide with a stanchion of the roof rack. Increasingly unnerved as he retrieves the keys, with trembling sweaty fingers he presses a tiny button on the ignition key and instantly hears twin metallic clunks as the door locks release. Carefully putting the keys into a front pocket of his shorts he takes a hold on the luggage rack and reaches down to the door handle, but within inches of grasping it pulls himself forward to get closer but raising his foot nudges the fishing rod toward the edge of the roof rack, frantically trying to stop it falling he watches it disappear, startling the basking reptiles it lands on to a thunderous chain reaction of hideous rattling.

JEFFREY – Shouting in blind panic as he scrambles back to the skylight.

"The plank is breaking, Luke, for god's sake get clear...GET CLEAR!"

CUT TO - LUKE - Rapidly stepping down from the skylight when he sees Jeffrey's legs appear as he clambers into the bedroom desperately straddling both lower bunks to slam the skylight closed and ram the bolt home. Sodden with sweat, his heart pounding, his hands trembling incessantly, with the terrifying roar diminishing Luke, badly shaken, sits and places a comforting arm around his father's shoulders, the sudden contact resulting in Jeffrey curtly pushing him away then to rapidly haul him into a despairing embrace. Gazing straight ahead in what combat veterans term a thousand-yard stare, Jeffrey retreats into the solace of imagining he's in his lounge as Lenny plays captivating melodies.

SCENE FADES...

OPENING SCENE

THE BEDROOM – SOMETIME LATER...

In the merciless heat now dominating the bedroom, as Jeffrey listens to music only he can hear staring at pictures only he can see, Luke, still in his father's arms, gazes forlornly at every item in the bedroom. When his attention rests first on Beric's stainless-steel bowl, then on commando dagger still wedged under the door, easing himself away from his father he goes to the utility cupboard and rummages around until he sees the binoculars. Nodding, and picking them up he walks to the door and begins jerking the dagger from side to side to loosen and withdraw it.

SCENE FADES...

OPENING SCENE

CUT TO – Jeffrey, still sat on a lower bunk, unshaven, gaunt, appearing ten years older, blinking several times before watching how Luke, sat on the opposite lower bunk is dismantling a front lens from the binoculars. Resting beside Luke Jeffrey sees Beric's steel water bowl containing what appears to be a small amount of ginger coloured hair.

LUKE - Casually glancing at his father and discarding the binoculars as he exclaims.

"DAD? You're OK!"

JEFFREY- Pensively murmuring.

"I don't know what the hell happened out there Luke, I was so close to entering the cab, but when that damn rod landed on the snakes, I panicked, I was stark terrified!"

JEFFREY. Hesitating, and glancing up at the skylight.

"I'll try again, the roof rack makes getting into the cab easy!"

LUKE – Insistently shaking his head.

"Dad, what happened to you would terrify anyone, you showed huge courage by what you did...!"

LUKE - Hesitating before adding.

"You're right when you say the only safe way out of this is getting to the cab, but you don't need to go back out there, I've figured a much safer way of doing it!"

JEFFREY – Murmuring disdainfully.

"SAFE? Right now son, there's no such thing as safe!"

LUKE – Adamantly.

"Dad, I'm telling you we've got everything we need right here to reach the cab!"

JEFFREY – Tolerantly.

"OK, I'm listening! Go right ahead!"

LUKE - Pausing to draw a long deep breath before stating.

"My idea is to smoke the snakes out of the lounge!"

JEFFREY - Scoffing incredulously.

"For god's sake Luke, what the hell are you saying?"

LUKE - Determinedly.

"DAD? At least listen to what I want to say?"

JEFFREY - Grudgingly...

"OK, go ahead, convince me?"

LUKE – Lifting Beric's bowl.

"What you see in this bowl is horsehair, the mattresses are stuffed with it, horsehair doesn't burn dad, it smoulders, more to the point gives off dense obnoxious smoke, my idea is to ignite it then push the bowl into the lounge, all snakes are blind, they see things on picture forming radar, when they sense smoke they'll almost certainly head for the sunlight in the door to avoid it!"

JEFFREY – Immediately contemptuous.

"Just like that?"

LUKE - Superbly confident

"Yes dad! Just like that!"

JEFFREY - Scathingly.

"LUKE, I see your logic, but have you thought about starting a real fire! It's too risky, the only way out of this is the roof!"

LUKE – Confidently persistent.

"DAD, look at this bowl, it's ten inches wide, six inches deep and made of stainless steel, if we only ignite this small amount of horsehair it will belch out plenty of toxic smoke and easily contain any risk of fire!"

JEFFREY – Suddenly hesitant.

"OK, suppose that works, how do we ignite it? The matches are in the lounge!"

LUKE - Placing the bowl down and lifting a front optical lens he's removed from the binoculars.

"We condense sunlight into the bowl through this!"

JEFFREY – Now visibly attentive.

"OK, so how do we get the bowl into the lounge?"

LUKE – Affirmatively.

"By carefully rehearsing it, there's a broom in the cupboard, when I start the smoke I place the bowl close to the door, you open it wide enough for me to push the bowl into the lounge, then slam the door when I pull the broom back!"

LUKE – Adding with massive emphasis.

"It's only four steps to the cab, we can cut up blankets for extra protection and we've got an endless supply of fishing line to tie it in place, we can do this dad, we CAN make it work!"

JEFFREY – Dubiously wiping his forehead.

"I reckon what you're proposing is little short of ingenious, but I want to see what pens if and when you ignite the horsehair!"

LUKE - Immediately pulling back a curtain.

"Watch!"

Placing the bowl in the narrow shaft of bright sunlight that enters the bedroom and directing it via the binocular lens into the bowl, within seconds a plume of arid black smoke spirals to the ceiling then rebounds down starting for man and boy a bout of violent coughing. While Luke quickly places the bowl on the floor, turning it upside down to smother then stamp out the horsehair, Jeffrey straddles both lower bunks, opening the skylight and briskly waving a blanket to clear the last of the foul-smelling fumes.

LUKE - When their coughing subsides.

"That was only a small amount of horsehair dad, imagine a full bowl in the lounge!"

JEFFREY – In sudden obvious awe.

"Luke, you've convinced me, but you say 'we' will go to the cab, there's no need for both of us to go, I'll go alone and..."

LUKE- Defiantly retorting.

"NO WAY Dad! NO WAY! We're in this together, we'll damn well get out of it together!"

JEFFREY - About to pull rank, reluctantly answering.

"OK, but I'll be in front, you will stay behind me until we reach the cab!"

SCENE FADES...
NEW SCENE - THE BEDROOM
VISUAL ONLY.

Glistening with sweat, yet with brisk teamwork, father and son meticulously practice getting the bowl into the lounge before layering each other with overlapping blankets secured with the inexhaustible orange fishing line. With their feverish preparations complete, Jeffrey eases the bedroom door open half an inch and rapidly pushes it closed.

LUKE - Not missing Jeffrey's fearful reaction.

"What?"

JEFFREY - Visibly unsure.

"There's a whole load of them piled up outside the door!"

LUKE – Insistently.

"DAD, we can't stop now! The door will only be open for split seconds, they won't come toward the smoke, they'll sense it and instinctively retreat.

JEFFREY - With mammoth apprehension.

"I hope your right son! I hope to God your right!"

CUT TO – Luke, half filling the bowl and igniting it, when it begins to smoulder he carefully places it beside the door and lines up the broom squarely behind it, when Jeffrey opens the door to the exact width of the bowl Luke gently nudges it toward the cluster of reptiles who, exactly as he said, begin rattling but collectively retreating. The instant Luke withdraws the broom, Jeffrey slams the door. The chilling manoeuvre takes mere seconds. As father and son endure a further bout of severe coughing, both waving blankets to eject the torrid smoke toward the skylight, beyond the door they hear frantic but diminishing rattling.

CUT TO - THE BASE OF THE DOOR.

Jeffrey, curtailing smoke wafting into the bedroom from under the door with a folded bed sheet he spreads along the base and stamps into an effective seal. By now, in the unrelenting heat, their moist faces now blackened as a residue of smoke clings to them, father and son are close to physical and mental exhaustion. Sitting opposite each other on the lower bunks listening for any slight sound beyond the bedroom door

Jeffrey clenches the remaining fishing rod, Luke, a spear he's made by securing his iconic dagger with fishing line to the shaft of the broom after removing the brush head.

JEFFREY – Pensively murmuring.

"It's really silent out there...?"

LUKE – Standing, taking a tight grip on his spear.

"It's four steps dad! Let's go for it!"

JEFFREY – Commandingly, as he scoops up and tosses the blanket seal to the rear of the bedroom.

"Before we go, breath in and hold it for as long as you can!"

When Luke nods, and they both strenuously inhale, Jeffrey cautiously opens the door and huddled together like silhouettes enter the dense black smoke in the lounge stepping around the still smouldering bowl and Beric's remains until Jeffrey's forward probing with the steel tip of the rod rebounds with the sound of metal on metal. Blindly groping a door handle and rapidly sliding both doors open Jeffrey enters the cab instantly turning haul Luke into it. Slamming both doors closed and sagging into their respective seats their frantic coughing suddenly becomes trivial that against all odds they've survived an ordeal in hell itself...

CUT TO – THE LOUNGE Showing a frying pan with several rashers of bacon sizzling.

CUT TO – JEFFREY – Sliding the pan away from the gas when he hears a sudden yelp coming from the bedroom.

CUT TO – THE BEDROOM.

Jeffrey enters the bedroom to see Luke sitting up in his bunk staring incredulously at a perfectly healthy Beric sat between the two lower bunks staring back at him. Suddenly pushing his bedding aside Luke scrambles down and hauls Jeffrey into an immense bear hug...

LUKE – As he cries.

"I love you dad, I love you!"

JEFFREY – Grinning.

"Hey? What's brought this on?"

Making no response, Luke releases his father and kneels, his arms opening for Beric to plod into them. Somewhat bemused Jeffrey returns to the lounge and slides the pan back onto the gas ring. Turning to glance into the bedroom, he sees Luke, a blink away from tears as he clings to his beloved Beric.

SCENE FADES.

CUT TO - NEW SCENE – EXTERIOR - BENEATH THE CANOPY. SOMETIME LATER.

CUT TO – Beric, alternating between father and son for an occasional bacon rind as they consume a fried breakfast.

JEFFREY - Pouring coffee, placing a mug in front of Luke.

"Nice to see the back of that mist!"

LUKE - Nodding agreeably as he gazes at the surrounding terrain swathed in glorious sunshine.

"Dad! Remember I told you about that competition in school to see who can write the best screenplay?"

JEFFREY – Curiously.

"Sure!"

LUKE - Briefly smiling.

"I've got the ending to an idea I've been writing on this vacation!"

JEFFREY – Inquiring.

"What's it about?"

LUKE – With a warm knowing smile...

"It's about two boys, one who drops a toy into a bucket of squirming fishing bait, and one who discovers how much his father really loves him!"

JEFFREY - Exuberantly.

"Well, I'll be damned! I can't wait to read it, when we finish breakfast I'll reverse back to the trail down the mountain, we'll stop at Clem's place to clean up and let him know we're OK, then, we'll make a straight run for home!"

LUKE - As he begins gathering dishes.

"Dad, when we're headed to Clems place, I want to sit in the lounge and make notes while scenes for my screenplay are clear in my head!"

JEFFREY - Grinning as he places his arm around Luke's shoulders.

"Sure Luke, absolutely no problem!"

SCENE FADES...

BRIEF NEW SCENE - SOMETIME LATER...

CUT TO - *The Screaming Eagle* crossing the desert track toward the distant highway.

NEW SCENE - CLEM HUDSON'S VERANDA

CUT TO - Clem, sat reading his book, standing when he looks up to see *The Screaming Eagle* approaching. Marking his page in his usual way before dropping the book on the table.

CLEM - Walking over to the RV as Jeffrey turns off the engine and climbs down.

"Welcome back! How did you get on at the Basin?"

JEFFREY- Grasping Clem's outstretched hand.

"It's a hell of a climb getting there, but well worth it, the views were everything you said they would be, we got caught in the mist you mentioned and went to ground for the night, we also had a run-in with a rattler!"

CLEM – Warily.

"A rattler! What happened?"

JEFFREY – Informatively.

"Our dog warned us, I shot it from twenty feet away!"

CLEM – Knowingly.

"Well you were dammed lucky! You rarely see a rattler in the wild until you hear it, and it's nailed you!"

JEFFREY - Nodding.

"I sure can't argue with that! We're headed home Clem, we stopped by to let you know we're OK, we'd like to pay for a quick shower before hitting the road?"

CLEM – Nodding.

"Help yourselves, but for letting me know you're both safe, the showers are on the house!"

CLEM -Smiling and turning back to his book.

"Be sure to tie your dog off and clean up after him!"

JEFFREY - Climbing into the cab and firing up the engine with a broad grin as he watches Clem sit and take up his book.

SCENE FADES…

NEW SCENE - LATER THAT DAY.

CUT TO - The RV's windscreen showing a green overhead sign indicating a turnoff for Phoenix.

LUKE – Contentedly holding Beric on his lap.

"Dad? What do you figure doing with this RV?"

JEFFREY - Shrugging.

"I was thinking of selling it back to the dealer, why?"

LUKE - Inquiringly…

"Can we leave it on the forecourt for a while, I'd like to sit in it and finish my screenplay!"

JEFFREY – Grinning and nodding.

"Keep it son, it's yours!"

After father and son exchange a spontaneous high five…

LUKE - Removing his cell phone from its charger.

JEFFREY – Curiously.

"Who are you calling?"

LUKE - Smiling with amusement.

"I'm calling mom, something I thought about last night, I'll convince her we're a hundred miles away and minutes later we'll surprise her!"

JEFFREY – Grinning.

"Cool Hand Luke! Is there no end to your brilliant ideas?"

LUKE – Smiling and shaking his head.

"No sir, there ain't!"

SCENE FADES…

NEW SCENE - JEFFREY'S HOME - LATE AFTERNOON.

CUT TO – Jeffrey home surrounded by the tranquil orange glow of a typical Arizona sunset.

CUT TO - Lenny on the front veranda wearing sandals, a yellow halter-neck top, a tan-coloured headscarf and white shorts. Beside her is a small table containing a large overgrown plant resting sideways in its pot for her to prune re-usable vines she drops into a round wicker basket on the floor. When her mobile suddenly rings she quickly discards her secateurs and gloves when she sees the caller is Luke.

LENNY – Exclaiming.

"Luke? Where are you? Are you both okay?"

CUT TO - THE CAB OF THE RV.

LUKE - Winking at Jeffrey.

"We're both fine Mom! We've had an amazing trip together, we're headed home, we're about a hundred miles away, we'll be with you in roughly two hours...!"

LENNY - Impatiently fumbling for the recall button when the call suddenly terminates, then drawn toward the end of drive when she sees the RV enter it.

CUT TO - MOMENTS LATER...

Amid a murderous rendition of "My Darling Clementine" from father and son the grime layered *Screaming Eagle* draws to a halt on the forecourt.

LENNY - Walking toward the RV with a huge, contented grin.

JEFFREY - Shutting down the engine and taking a hold of Beric's collar as Luke scrambles down to run into Lenny's wide-open arms. Releasing Beric moments later for him to leap from the cab for Luke to calm him when he meets Lenny. Moving to the lounge, Jeffrey scoops up his Winchester from the washroom and exiting via the side door slams it closed then turns to see his wife and son, arm in arm, gazing adoringly at him.

CUT TO – LENNY - staring at Jeffrey, her expressions conveying how suntanned and ruggedly handsome he looks, that he's lost weight, and what the hell has he done to his expensive designer jeans.

JEFFREY - Not for a moment taking his eyes from Lenny as he halts in front of her murmuring with massive feeling.

"Len, you look...absolutely stunning!"

Drawing her into his arms, Luke obligingly takes the Winchester from him.

CUT TO – A re-united family walking toward the house, plodding contentedly behind them is the family dog.

SCENES FADES...

CONCLUDING SCENE...

CUT TO – Inside the house, which is silent and dark. A clock on a mantlepiece with luminous numbers shows the time is two am.

CUT TO - JEFFREY - Sound asleep with Lenny nestled into his shoulder.

LUKE - Also asleep, with Beric sleeping at the end of his bed.

CUT TO – The forecourt, vaguely illuminated by a light on the veranda roof.

CUT TO - *The Screaming Eagle.* It's engine long cooled, not radiating any sound.

CUT TO – A drainage hole in the circular compartment holding a spare wheel beneath the RV where a small rattlesnake slowly emerges then drops onto the cold surface of the forecourt. Moving onto the veranda it senses the familiar odour of foliage in Lenny's wicker basket. Forming itself into a coil as it nestles into the basket it briefly emits the rattle, the hideous sound able to terrifying the bravest of men...

The End...?

Don't miss out!

Visit the website below and you can sign up to receive emails whenever Barrie David publishes a new book. There's no charge and no obligation.

https://books2read.com/r/B-A-NCTG-VSRLC

BOOKS2READ

Connecting independent readers to independent writers.

Also by Barrie David

Luke Blake's Screenplay
Memories of Mileage Past
Journey to Prague and other Mileage

About the Author

As a life long lover of books and writing, I am contentedly enjoying my retirement and live in the Vale of Glamorgan - South Wales with my wife Elly and our dog Enzo and cat Molly.

I love passing on my life experiences to others.

About the Publisher

Currently retired and living in the Vale of Glamogan - South Wales with my wife Elly plus our dog Enzo and cat Molly I enjoy writing and sharing my experiences with others.